DINK, JOSH, AND RUTH ROSE
AREN'T THE ONLY KID DETECTIVES!

WHAT ABOUT YOU?

CAN YOU FIND THE HIDDEN MESSAGE INSIDE THIS BOOK?

There are 26 illustrations in this book, not counting the one on the title page, the map at the beginning, and the picture of the dinosaur skull that repeats at the start of many of the chapters. In each of the 26 illustrations, there's a hidden letter. If you can find all the letters, you will spell out a secret message!

If you're stumped, the answer is on the bottom of page 133.

HAPPY DETECTING!

This is dedicated to my young readers.
You are my inspiration!
—R.R.

To Payton, Abigail, and Jolie
—J.S.G.

ISBN 978-1-338-30043-7

12 11 10 9 8 7 6 5 4 3 2 1   18 19 20 21 22 23

Printed in the U.S.A.   40

First Scholastic printing, April 2018

A to Z Mysteries®

SUPER EDITION 10

Colossal Fossil

by Ron Roy

illustrated by
John Steven Gurney

SCHOLASTIC INC.

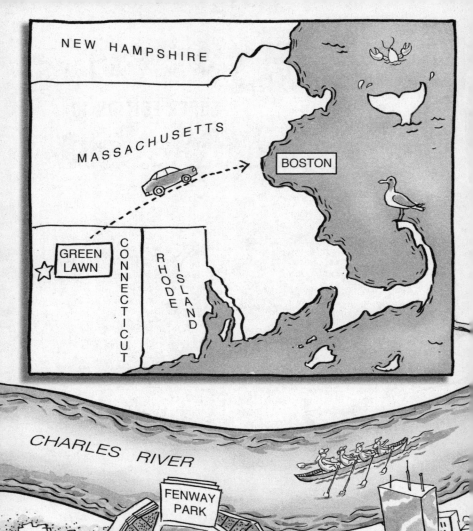

NEW HAMPSHIRE

MASSACHUSETTS

BOSTON

GREEN LAWN

CONNECTICUT

RHODE ISLAND

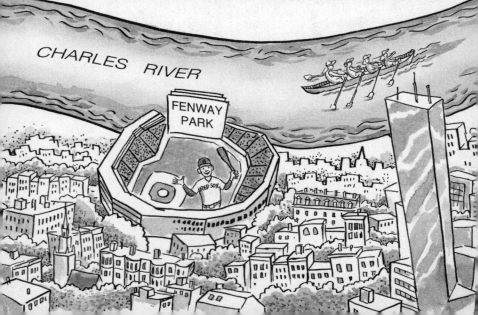

CHARLES RIVER

FENWAY PARK

RED SOX

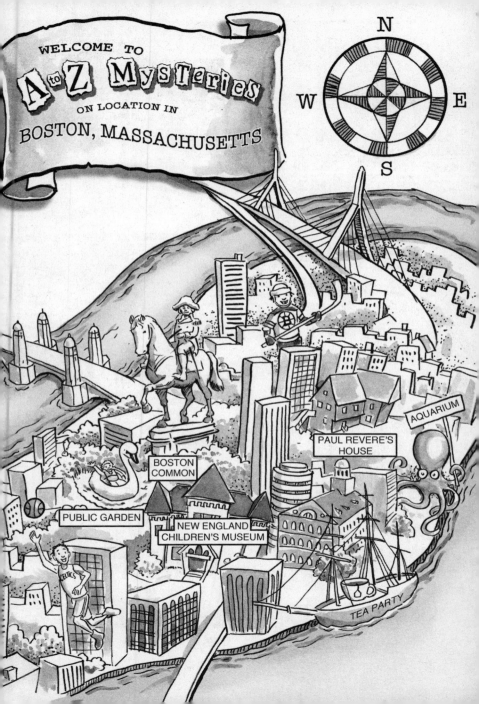

CHAPTER 1

"I can't believe we're sleeping in a museum tonight," Josh said. "I saw a movie once where some kids stayed overnight in a museum, and no one ever saw them again!"

Dink grinned at Josh. "What happened to them?" he asked.

"A dinosaur ate them!"

"If no one ever saw the kids again," Dink asked, "how do you know a dinosaur got them?"

"The police found bloody dinosaur tracks in the museum!" Josh said.

Ruth Rose laughed. "This museum

has dinosaurs," she said, "but they've been dead for a long time. Nothing to worry about!"

Dink, Josh, and Ruth Rose were in Boston, Massachusetts, with Dink's father. He had a business meeting there and had brought the kids with him. They were in the Boston Public Garden, where they planned to visit the New England Children's Museum. During the year, the museum invited kids for special sleepovers. Dink's dad had signed them up a week ago.

The kids wore backpacks and carried their rolled-up sleeping bags. As they hiked past a pond in the Public Garden, Dink watched people riding in boats that had giant carved swans at the back.

"That looks like fun!" Ruth Rose said. "I'd like to try it."

"Do those boats ever tip over?" Josh asked.

Mr. Duncan laughed. "I don't think so," he said. "But you'd be in shallow water, and you could walk right out onto the lawn."

"I see the museum!" Ruth Rose said, pointing straight ahead.

In the shade of a giant pine tree stood a stone building with lots of windows. The museum was set in a lawn with shrubbery and hundreds of yellow daffodils moving in the breeze. A sign over the wide front door said NEW ENGLAND CHILDREN'S MUSEUM—A LEARNING PLACE.

A crowd of kids and parents were standing near the museum entrance. Some of the kids were wearing costumes. One boy was all in black, with four extra arms sewn onto his black sweatshirt. "Look," Dink said to Josh and Ruth Rose. "A giant spider!"

Josh shuddered. "I'm glad he's not real," he said.

"But there are real ones inside," Ruth

Rose teased. "There's a spider exhibit, and I'm dying to see it!"

Two younger kids were wearing green dinosaur costumes. They looked like twins. The boy's T-shirt said I'M FRED. His sister's said I'M RUBY. They each held a teddy bear under one arm. They carried sleeping bags, like everyone else.

A small banner next to the door read COME INSIDE AND MEET OUR COLOSSAL FOSSIL!

Just then a woman stepped out through the door. She wore a blue shirt with the museum's initials, NECM, printed on the front; a baseball cap; and cargo pants.

She knelt near a man who was sitting on the ground, leaning against the trunk of the pine tree.

The man had on raggedy pants and a ripped winter jacket. A ski cap was pulled over his tangled gray hair. Next to him lay a brown dog. The dog's tail wagged when the woman patted him on the head.

She handed the man a small lunch bag. He looked inside the bag and pulled out a sandwich, then tore off the wrapping and took a big bite. The woman went back to the museum steps and smiled at the people waiting.

"I'm Sylvia Slate," she said. "I'm one of your chaperones for tonight. Come on in!"

They all trooped through the doorway. A long table had been set up inside the lobby, where museum workers were checking off names. Then Sylvia and more chaperones in blue shirts led everyone into a small auditorium. "Please find a seat, folks!" Sylvia called out. She was standing on a stage. The kids and their parents filled in a few rows of seats.

She introduced the other chaperones: "Say hi to Tyler, Sandy, Trish, and

Otto!" The four chaperones waved, and the kids and parents clapped.

Just then a man ran through the auditorium and leaped onto the stage. He had curly black hair and a black beard. He was wearing what looked like an animal skin covered with long black hair. He was carrying a club, and leather sandals were tied onto his feet. "What about me?" he said.

Sylvia laughed. "Oh yes, I forgot our caveman," she said. "Say hi to Nog!"

"Hi, Nog!" everyone called out.

Nog bowed. "Hi right back at you!" he yelled in a deep voice.

"Do you really live in a cave?" a kid yelled, and everyone laughed.

Nog grinned. "Nope. I live in a nice apartment here in Boston, right across the street from Paul Revere's house."

"Who's Paul Revere?" the same kid asked.

His father smiled and said, "I'll tell you later, Brian."

"Nog is going to show you some of the museum exhibits," Sylvia told the group. "Then we'll split up into smaller groups, and you'll get to choose one of us as your personal chaperone for the evening!"

Nog waved his club in the air. "Make a long line and follow me!" he said.

"Leave your sleeping bags and back-packs here," Sylvia called out. "You'll pick them up again later."

For the next half hour, Nog led the group around parts of the museum. They saw a Triceratops that Nog told them was twenty-three feet long. "This guy's skeleton was found in South Dakota," he said.

The kids and adults stared up at the huge skeleton.

"No touching!" Nog called out when little Fred put a finger on the skeleton's leg. "He's ticklish!"

Nog took them past a room where small animals lived. Another room on the tour was filled with birds in cages. A few of the birds were sleeping, but most were cheeping and chirping.

"Look, butterflies!" one kid yelled when Nog showed them a huge room filled with flowers and trees. Thousands of colorful butterflies flew about.

They saw a room where you could study germs under microscopes. A sign on the window said WHAT MAKES YOU SICK? COME IN AND LEARN!

"And here's our spider room," Nog said. He grinned through his thick beard. "I hope you don't all have nightmares tonight!"

They looked through a large window and saw a bunch of cages. In one cage, a big tarantula clung to the wire.

"Can we go in?" Ruth Rose asked. "My friend Josh just loves spiders!"

"You can do that later with your chaperone," Nog said. "Now it's time to get a snack. But before we do, I want you to come and meet Spino!"

"I hope Spino isn't another spider!" Josh whispered to Dink.

"Spino is our colossal fossil!" Nog said. He led them to a tall room with windows near the ceiling.

Dink felt a breeze. He thought he

could smell the flowers outside the building.

In one wall of the room were two doors, labeled OFFICE and LABORATORY in black letters. The laboratory door was partly open, and Dink saw a man inside, peering through a microscope.

In the middle of the tall room was a roped-off area. Behind the ropes stood the partly constructed skeleton of a dinosaur. It had a long neck and tail. Plastic plants and painted cardboard rocks made the ground under the skeleton look like a riverbed. There was even artificial water, which Dink thought was probably plastic painted to look like a river.

"This is Spino," Nog told the group. "Real name, Spinosaurus. He was found by a farmer in Africa."

"Spino is awesome!" one of the kids said.

Nog pointed his club at the skeleton.

"He certainly is," he said. "This colossal fossil walked on the earth millions of years before people did. So I never had to worry about getting eaten by a dinosaur!"

They all gawked at the enormous dinosaur. "The museum scientists haven't finished putting the skeleton together yet," Nog went on. "The rest of the bones are still packed in those crates." He pointed to several large wooden boxes. A few workers were pulling out bones and laying them on the floor. Two other workers stood on ladders, doing something to the dinosaur's neck.

"What are those steel poles for?" Dink asked.

"The poles hold the skeleton up," Nog answered. "Without them, it might fall over. When the workers are done, Spino will stand balanced on his hind legs and tail. Then some of the poles will be removed."

They watched a man climb a ladder.

He stepped onto one of the wood planks
that ran between two more ladders. The
man stretched a tape measure along one
of the dinosaur's ribs, then wrote something in a notebook.

"Why do you call him Spino?" a girl asked.

"These dinosaurs had tall spines growing out of their backs, sort of like a sail," Nog explained. He pointed to an artist's drawing of Spinosaurus, the way it might have looked when it was alive. The drawing showed Spinosaurus standing at the edge of a river. The artist had painted other prehistoric animals into the scene, but Spino was the biggest.

Next to the drawing, a small sign read MEET SPINO, A TRULY COLOSSAL FOSSIL!

"How did you get the skeleton all the way from Africa to Boston?" Dink asked Nog.

"The museum bought the bones from the farmer who discovered them on his land," Nog explained. "Then our scientists joined their scientists to dig it all up, put it in special crates, and ship it here. The whole operation was very expensive!"

"You paid money for old bones?" Josh asked.

Nog smiled. "Yep," he said. "A *lot* of money. That's why our museum workers are being so careful as they put Spino together. This is a very valuable dinosaur!"

"He's so big!" Ruth Rose said.

"Yes, even larger than the T. rex," Nog said. "See his skull? Looks sort of like a crocodile's, doesn't it? His long jaws and sharp teeth helped Spino catch fish and other small creatures he liked to eat."

"Small creatures like *you*," Dink whispered into Josh's ear.

CHAPTER 2

Just then two men stepped out of the office and approached the group. One man had gray hair, wore a suit, and carried a briefcase. The man with him was much younger. His hair was red, and it was tied back in a ponytail. He was wearing jeans and a sweatshirt.

The older man smiled at Nog.

"This is Dr. Wurst," Nog told the group. "He's the museum director."

Dr. Wurst nodded at the kids and adults. "Welcome to the museum and our spring sleepover," he said. "I know that Nog and our other staff will make every effort to show you a good time!"

The man with the red ponytail smiled. "I hope you get a chance to see my River Diamond," he said. Then he and Dr. Wurst hurried away.

"What's the River Diamond?" a boy with thick glasses asked.

"Follow me!" Nog said. He pointed his club toward a small fenced-in area a few yards from the end of Spino's tail. Inside the black fencing stood a wooden pedestal with a clear dome on top. A light on the ceiling shone down on the dome. Inside, on a red cloth, was an object a little bigger than a tennis ball. It was covered with dark brown dirt, with shiny black parts showing through the dirt.

"This is the River Diamond!" Nog said. "The man you just saw with Dr. Wurst is Edward Alanis. He owns the diamond, and he lent it to the museum."

Everyone peered at the thing under the dome. "I thought diamonds were supposed to be shiny," Ruby said. "This is all dirty."

"It looks like the hunks of coal my grandparents had in their basement," her mom said.

Nog laughed. "You would be lucky to find *this* in your basement!" he said. "The River Diamond looks the way it did when Mr. Alanis pulled it from the mud

a few months ago. We left it just the way he found it, but under that goop is a very rare black diamond. When the diamond is returned to Mr. Alanis, he'll have a jeweler clean the mud away. Then the jeweler will polish the black diamond and cut it up into many smaller pieces. Each new diamond will be worth a lot of money."

"How much?" the boy with the glasses asked.

"Just as you see it here, the uncut diamond is worth at least five million dollars," Nog said. "Much more after it's been cleaned and cut up."

"Five million dollars?" Josh yelped. "Is that why there's a fence around it?"

"Yes," Nog answered. "If anyone touches the dome, a very sensitive alarm will go off."

The boy wearing glasses pulled a magnifying glass out of his pocket. He leaned over the fence and peered at the diamond.

"Not too close, please," Nog said. "We wouldn't want to set off that alarm!" Nog gently led the boy away from the diamond. "Now, let's go meet your chaperones and see where you're going to sleep tonight."

Everyone followed Nog past Spino's long tail bones to the other end of the big room. In the corner were two bathrooms, "His" and "Hers." Five feet from the bathrooms was a wide door opening into another space. This room had a blue carpet on the floor. Fans in two of the corners made a soft whirring sound. A cloth-covered table stood against one wall. Platters were arranged on the table, next to dishes, bottles of water, and silverware.

Dink noticed a movie projector and screen in another corner.

The chaperone named Sylvia walked over to the group. "How was your tour?" she asked.

"Cool!" Josh said. "Except for the spiders!"

"Why don't you all sit down?" Sylvia said. "Now is when you get to pick your personal chaperones. Then you can get your sleeping bags and bring them back here."

Everyone sat on the carpet. The other four chaperones stood in front of them. Nog left the group and walked back to the Spino exhibit. Dink could see the skeleton through the open door.

One chaperone raised his hand. "Hi, I'm Tyler. I love butterflies, and I'll show them to you later. Who wants to be in my group?"

A bunch of hands went up.

"Great, then follow me!" Tyler said. Some kids and their parents went with Tyler to a corner of the room.

Sandy raised her hand next. "My name is Sandy, and I can teach you about electricity. Stand up if you want to be in my group!"

About ten kids and adults followed Sandy to another corner.

After Trish and Otto were chosen by more kids, Sylvia was left. "Okay, I guess the rest of you are stuck with me!" she said.

"No, we wanted you!" Ruth Rose said. She, Dink, Josh, and Dink's father would be part of her group.

"Me too!" a boy called out. He was the one with the thick eyeglasses. He had been looking through his magnifying glass at the River Diamond in the other room.

The boy was with his father. "I'm Greg Davis," the tall man said, "and this is my son, Alex Davis."

"And I'm Leanna Walker," the twins' mom said. "These little dinosaurs are

Fred and Ruby, as you can see by their T-shirts."

Dink's father introduced himself, Dink, Josh, and Ruth Rose.

"Great, six kids and three adults, a nice small group," Sylvia said. "Let's go get your sleeping bags and stuff. We'll be sleeping right here in this room. Then we'll have supper and watch a movie."

"Can we sleep in the room with Spino?" Ruby asked. "I love dinosaurs!"

"Sorry, that room is off-limits," Sylvia said. "But we'll be very close! You can see Spino from this room, right through the door!"

Sylvia was wearing a bracelet made out of beads, colored stones, and chunks of metal. She pushed a tiny button, making the top of one of the pieces of metal pop open. Inside was a watch face. "It's six o'clock," she said. "After the movie, you can choose an exhibit you'd like to see before bedtime."

"I love your bracelet!" Ruth Rose said.

Sylvia held her wrist out so Ruth Rose could get a better look. "I made it myself," she said. "I create jewelry in my spare time. Someday I hope to sell my things online."

"I'd buy one!" Ruth Rose said.

All five chaperones led their kids out to retrieve their sleeping bags and backpacks. Everyone came back in to choose spots on the floor.

"Pick a space for your sleeping bags," Sylvia told her nine charges. "If you need the bathrooms, they're right outside the door."

She pointed up at the exit sign above the door. "The exit sign is lit, so no one should have a problem finding the door. And those small lights on the walls stay on all night. I'll dim them low when we go to sleep."

She dropped her own sleeping bag next to the door.

"Let's go over by that wall," Dink's father suggested. "I can read under the lights."

The kids dragged their backpacks and sleeping bags to the back of the room. Mr. Davis and Alex did the same. Ms. Walker and the twins laid down their sleeping bags about twenty feet away.

Dink's father chose a spot under a light. He pulled a book of crossword puzzles from his backpack.

Dink, Josh, and Ruth Rose unrolled their sleeping bags in a row. They were about thirty feet from the exit door, where Sylvia was getting settled on her bag.

"Cool," Ruth Rose said. "We can see Spino from here."

Dink grinned at Josh. "I hope he doesn't get hungry during the night for Josh ice cream!" he said.

"Or Dink soup," Josh said.

Dink's father was talking with Mr. Davis. Alex was a few feet away, reading a book.

"I think Alex would rather read than eat," Mr. Davis said. "His backpack is filled with books!"

Mr. Davis looked at Mr. Duncan's book. "I see you like doing crosswords," he said. He pulled a paperback book from his pack. "Ever do any anagrams?"

"I do like anagrams, but I never seem to have the time," Dink's father said.

"And I like crosswords, too," Mr. Davis said. "Why don't we swap books for tonight?"

The two dads exchanged books, and Mr. Davis went over to join his son.

Dink pointed to the book his father was holding. "What's an anagram?" he asked.

"An anagram is a word or phrase made from rearranging the letters in another word or phrase," he said. "For example, look at the word *ANAGRAM* on this book cover. If you rearrange those seven letters, you can make *NAG A RAM*."

"Cool!" Josh said.

Dink's father turned to Ruth Rose. "The eight letters in your name can become *REST HOUR* or *HERO RUST*," he told her.

The three kids laughed.

"Can you do my name?" Josh asked.

"Sorry, *JOSH* doesn't work," Mr. Duncan said. "But your last name, *PINTO*, can make *POINT, IN POT,* or *TOP IN*."

"How about my name?" Dink asked.

His father handed the book to him. "See if you can figure it out yourself," he said. "Don't lose the book—I have to return it to Alex's dad in the morning."

Just then Sylvia rang a little bell. "Who's hungry?" she called out.

CHAPTER 3

Everyone yelled back, "Me!"

"That's great! Now make a line and help yourselves," Sylvia said. "Be sure to take a dino cookie!"

The platters held hamburgers and veggie burgers. There was a bowl of salad, and another holding fresh fruit. Next to the fruit was a plate of cookies shaped like little dinosaurs.

Everyone filled a plate, grabbed a bottle of water, and headed back to their sleeping bags. The room got pretty noisy with people eating, talking, and laughing.

"That was great," Josh said twenty minutes later. His plate was empty.

"Looks like there are plenty of cookies left," Dink's father said. He gave Josh a nudge. "Why don't you go over and get more?"

"I guess I could eat one more cookie," Josh said as he headed toward the long table.

"The movie will start in five minutes!" Sylvia called out to the room. "Toss your trash, please, and be sure to put your water bottles in the recycling barrel."

All around the room, the groups of kids and chaperones made themselves comfortable on their sleeping bags. Some of the parents were chatting with each other.

Sylvia flipped a wall switch and the room went dark. Everyone got quiet.

Josh came back with some dinosaur cookies on a paper plate. The three kids sat on their sleeping bags and munched cookies.

The movie was about a young dinosaur who got lost. He escaped some meat-eating dinosaurs and fell into a rushing river. But his mother found him, so there was a happy ending.

Everyone clapped and yelled when the movie was over.

Sylvia turned up the lights. "Okay, who's ready for some more fun?" she called out.

Lots of voices shouted, "Yay!"

"Your chaperones are going to take

you all on a secret adventure!" Sylvia said. "Tyler, Sandy, Trish, and Otto, are you ready?"

"We're ready!" the four chaperones called back. They led their groups of kids and parents out of the room. There was lots of giggling and chattering. Some of the kids were in stocking feet.

"Where are *we* going?" Alex asked Sylvia when the others had left.

"Secret," Sylvia said. She led her group of nine out of the room, past Spino and the River Diamond. Fred and Ruby Walker carried their teddy bears with them.

"How about a hint?" Mr. Davis asked Sylvia.

"Okay," Sylvia said. "Think wet but also dry, big and small, colorful and plain!"

"No fair!" Josh said. "That could be anything!"

Sylvia just smiled. They all followed

her up a set of stairs and down a corridor, and stopped at a black door. "Everyone needs to stay quiet," she said in a low voice. "We don't want to scare our friends!"

"What friends?" Alex asked.

"Frogs!" Sylvia said. She opened the door and ushered in her charges.

"Oh my gosh!" Ruth Rose said. All around them were pools, aquariums, and cages filled with frogs. There were tiny green ones, huge brown ones, and even bright blue ones.

They made different sounds, from chirping to what sounded like burping. One variety let out low whistles. Some of the frogs swam in water, and others sat on rocks or lily pads.

"They come from all over the world," Sylvia said. "The little blue ones are from Japan!"

She showed them a pool where a bunch of different frogs lived. "You can put your hands in there," she said. "These frogs don't mind being held—just do it gently."

Everyone gathered around the pool and stuck their hands in. "Ooh, I touched one!" Ruby said.

Dink picked up a giant bullfrog. It was dark green with a soft white belly. The frog's long back legs wiggled around, tickling Dink's hands.

After about twenty minutes, Sylvia said, "Okay, bedtime for frogs and kids! Let's head back."

They followed her past darkened rooms. One had a sign on the door that read LET'S PLANT A GARDEN! Through the window, Dink saw Sandy and her group.

Back in the sleeping room, almost everyone had returned from their adventure. Kids and adults were getting into their sleeping bags. Most of the kids wore their regular clothes, but Fred and Ruby were wearing jammies.

Soon the room was quiet.

Dink's dad and Mr. Davis were

talking softly, leaning against the wall under one of the dimmed lights.

Josh and Ruth Rose kicked off their shoes and crawled inside their sleeping bags.

"Josh?" Dink whispered.

"What?"

"I don't mean to scare you," he said, "but I think I saw an enormous spider crawling into your sleeping bag."

"Very unfunny, sonny," Josh said. Then he rolled over and pretended to snore.

Dink snuggled into his sleeping bag. A few minutes later he was asleep. He dreamed that he was a cave boy. His blond hair was long and tangled. He wore an animal skin and no shoes. He slept in a cave and made pets out of baby wild animals.

In his dream, Dink was fishing in a river when a big black creature rose out of the water. It had sharp teeth and long black hair. The monster grabbed Dink and began licking his face. Its breath smelled like rotten fish.

Dink woke up. His heart was beating fast, and he felt too warm inside the sleeping bag. He unzipped it and peeled off his sweatshirt. Everyone else was asleep. Snoring sounds came from his dad's sleeping bag.

I'm safe, he told himself. *No hairy monsters.*

Closing his eyes again, Dink drifted into sleep.

Suddenly a loud crash made him sit up. Then an alarm went off, like the ones Dink had heard on ambulances. The sound wailed through the room, waking everyone. Fred and Ruby began to cry. Dink heard their mother trying to comfort them.

Everyone was sitting up, climbing out of their sleeping bags. The chaperones

and parents were yelling back and forth. Nobody knew what was happening, or what made the alarm continue to shriek.

"What's going on?" Josh asked as his head popped out of his sleeping bag. His hair was spiky and his eyes were big.

The alarm sound was coming from the Spinosaurus room. Dink looked toward the door. Sylvia wasn't there. Her sleeping bag was empty.

The Walker kids were still crying. The alarm kept bleating. "Is it a fire drill?" Mr. Davis yelled. "Should we get out of here?"

The alarm suddenly stopped, and Sylvia appeared in the doorway. She looked scared. "Sorry about the racket," she said with a shaky voice. "There's been an accident!"

CHAPTER 4

"What happened, Sylvia?" Dink's father asked.

"It's Spino," she said. "Something fell. I'm going to call Dr. Wurst." She turned and hurried out.

The sleeping room got very loud. Everyone was talking or yelling. The twins cuddled with their mom on her sleeping bag. Alex and his dad came over and began talking with Dink's father.

"Let's go check it out," Josh said.

Dink, Josh, and Ruth Rose walked over and peeked through the door. The Spino skeleton was still standing, but one of the long planks had fallen away. One end of the heavy plank had landed on the painting of Spino, smashing it. A tall ladder was also flat on the floor.

Eight feet away, the other end of the plank had knocked over the River Diamond display case. The pedestal was broken, and the dome was on the floor.

In their socks, Dink, Josh, and Ruth Rose stepped around splinters of wood. Dink walked over to the dome and peeked inside. It was empty. "Where's the River Diamond?" he asked.

"It probably just rolled somewhere when the dome fell over," Ruth Rose said. "Let's look around."

The three kids searched the floor between Spino's massive legs. Some of the fake plants had also been squashed under the heavy board. Dink looked among the plants and artificial rocks. He didn't see anything that looked like the River Diamond.

"Is that it?" Ruth Rose asked. She ran over to one end of the long plank. The River Diamond was on the floor under the board, wedged tight. She tried to pull the diamond out from under it.

"It's stuck under the board, and the board is real heavy," Ruth Rose said.

Dink put a hand on the wood plank and tried to shove it aside. "This thing weighs a ton, but we can probably move it together," he said.

The three kids knelt down and placed their hands on the plank. "SHOVE!" Dink said. It barely moved.

"Try again," Dink said. This time he leaned his shoulder against the rough wood as they shoved. The plank slid a few inches, and the diamond was free.

As Dink reached for it, a loud voice yelled, "WHAT DO YOU THINK YOU'RE DOING?"

The kids whipped around and looked into the angry face of Dr. Wurst.

Sylvia was standing next to him, looking worried.

Dink tried to swallow, but his mouth was dry.

"We were just trying to get the River Diamond," Ruth Rose said, pointing to the plank. "When the board crashed down, it got stuck un—"

"Yes, I can see that," Dr. Wurst said. He was wearing a purple tracksuit and sneakers that weren't tied. His gray hair spiked out on one side, like he'd just gotten out of bed.

By now, everyone else was crowded

around Spino and the fallen plank. They looked sleepy and surprised and scared. Dink felt his father's hand on his shoulder.

"Thank you, but we'll take care of this," Dr. Wurst announced. "Sylvia, would you mind?"

She stepped forward and scooped up the River Diamond, and she and Dr. Wurst walked into his office. The door closed, and Dink heard the lock click into place.

Two men in gray uniforms entered the room. One had a cell phone to his ear. He listened, nodded, and said, "Yes, sir!"

The other guard said, "Looks like the ladder fell against that plank, and the plank came loose and hit the floor. Okay, folks, you can go back to sleep now. We'll get our crew to clean up this mess."

Everyone left the room and returned to their sleeping bags. Alex held his father's hand. "I'm glad Spino didn't get broken!" he said.

"I'm glad, too," his father said.

Dink, Josh, and Ruth Rose sat on Ruth Rose's sleeping bag. She turned on her flashlight and stood it between them. The light turned their faces into Halloween masks.

"Try to get some sleep," Dink's father called quietly as he lay on his sleeping bag. He checked his watch. "It's three in the morning!"

"Okay, Dad," Dink said. "Good night."

"What's that on your shirt?" Josh asked Dink.

"Where?" Dink asked, looking down.

"On your shoulder, dude." Josh leaned over and plucked something off Dink's T-shirt. He held his fingers over the flashlight beam. "Gross, it looks like hair!"

"Let me see," Dink said, reaching for Josh's fingers. "You're right. It's hair. Three hairs."

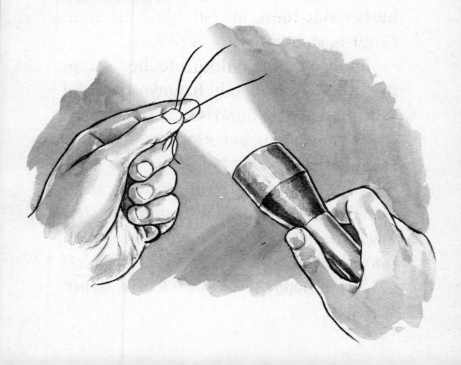

Dink suddenly remembered his nightmare about the hairy black monster. He swallowed hard. *If I was just dreaming, how did those hairs get on my shirt?* he wondered.

"The hairs didn't come from you," Josh said. "They're black."

"It's probably my hair," Ruth Rose said. "When we were shoving that plank, I must have rubbed against you, Dink."

Dink shone the flashlight on the hairs. "But these are straight," he said. "Your hair is curly."

Ruth Rose crawled into her sleeping bag. "Then it's a hairy mystery," she said. "Good night, guys."

"You mean good night *again*," Josh said from inside his bag.

Dink stared at the hairs for a minute. They were real, not from a monster. *Who has straight black hair?* he asked himself. *And how did they get on my shirt?*

Too sleepy to think clearly, Dink

tucked the hairs inside the cover of
the anagram book. He'd think about
it tomorrow. Yawning, he shut off the
flashlight and burrowed into his bag.

Before he closed his eyes, Dink saw
Sylvia step back into the sleeping room.
She kicked off her shoes before crawling
inside her sleeping bag.

Under the glow from the exit light,
Dink noticed that Sylvia's hair was
straight and black. He fell asleep thinking about that.

CHAPTER 5

"Good morning, everyone!" Sylvia called out. She was standing behind the food table, holding a glass of orange juice.

Dink opened his eyes and blinked. The lights were bright, and he smelled something that made his stomach rumble. He sat up and stretched. The anagram book slid off his sleeping bag to the carpet.

Dink reached over and poked Josh's sleeping bag. "Josh, wake up! Someone stole all the food!" he whispered.

Josh's head popped out of the bag. "You'd better be teasing," he growled.

"Would I tease you?" Dink asked. He grabbed his backpack and headed for the bathroom. Mr. Davis and Alex were just coming out. Alex had toothpaste on his lips.

"Quite a night, wasn't it?" Mr. Davis said to Dink. Alex walked over to the River Diamond, which was back inside the dome on top of the pedestal. The fence was in place, and someone had swept the floor.

"I'm glad no one was standing near Spino when that board fell," Dink said.

"Righto," Mr. Davis said.

In the bathroom, Dink was surprised to see a man combing his hair at one of the sinks.

The guy noticed Dink and smiled. "Hi!" he said. "You must be with the sleepover. Enjoying it?"

"It's been great," Dink said. "Until the alarm went off last night."

"Yeah, bummer," the man said. "Oh,

I'm Trevor. I'm the museum paleontologist, which means I study fossils. I
started out as a police detective, then
decided I'd rather look for dinosaur clues
than crooks."

"I'm Dink Duncan," Dink said. "I'm
here with my dad and two of my friends."
He unzipped his backpack and took out
his toothbrush and toothpaste.

Trevor waved good-bye and left.

Dink stood in front of the mirror

and began brushing his teeth. Rinsing his mouth, he noticed a dark hair on the sink where Trevor had been standing. He took a closer look. The hair looked the same as the straight black hairs Josh had pulled off his shirt last night.

Dink gently wrapped the new hair in a paper towel and stuck it in a pocket. Then he pulled a clean T-shirt from his backpack. As he tugged the one he'd been wearing over his head, he felt something stick his ear. He ran his fingers over the cloth and found a wood splinter.

Dink plucked out the sliver. It was pointy as a needle. *When did I rub against something made of wood?* he asked himself. Then he remembered shoving the plank off the River Diamond last night. He figured that the sliver must have stuck in his shirt while they were moving the plank.

Then he realized that the sliver was in the exact same place where the hairs had been on his shirt. Which meant that the hairs probably came from the plank, too. But how did the hairs get onto the plank?

Dink tugged on the clean T-shirt and combed his hair with his fingers. He decided that maybe one of the museum workers had rubbed his head against the plank, leaving behind the three hairs.

But the workers all wore hard hats, didn't they?

Josh rushed into the bathroom. "Dude, they've got pancakes!" he said.

"Awesome. I'm starving," Dink said.

"And scrambled eggs and sausage!"

Dink left the bathroom while Josh was brushing his teeth. The ladder that had fallen was now leaning against a wall. The plank was once again high up, making a bridge between two sturdy ladders.

"Morning, Spino," Dink said as he walked past the skeleton. In the sleeping room, he dropped his backpack and hurried over to the breakfast table. Sylvia and the other chaperones were helping people fill up their plates. Ms. Walker was in line ahead of Dink. Dink noticed that her hair was light brown. Her two little kids were still in jammies. Their hair was blond.

Dink took a plate from the stack. "Eggs, Dink?" Sylvia asked. She was wearing the bracelet that Ruth Rose liked. The chunks of stone and metal clinked when she moved her arm.

"Yes, please, and a couple of pancakes, too," Dink said. Sylvia spooned some eggs onto his plate, then added two pancakes.

He felt something poke his back. "This is a stickup!" a hoarse voice whispered. "Gimme your pancakes!"

Dink turned around and saw Josh's grinning face. "I'm so hungry I could eat a dinosaur," he said.

"Better than the other way around," Ruth Rose said.

She liked to wear all one color. Yesterday, she'd worn all blue. Today, she had on orange pants and an orange sweatshirt and headband. Even her socks and sneakers were orange.

Dink laughed. He poured syrup over everything, grabbed an apple juice, and headed toward his sleeping bag. His father was sitting with Mr. Davis, so Dink joined them. A few minutes later, Josh and Ruth Rose carried their plates over.

"Where's Alex?" Dink's father asked Mr. Davis.

"Over there, behind an open book," Mr. Davis said. He grinned. "The kid is always reading and making plans. He can't decide if he wants to become a writer or a gemologist. Last week he wanted to be a detective."

"What's a gemologist?" Josh asked.

"Someone who studies gems," Mr. Davis said. "Alex is nuts about rubies, diamonds, and emeralds. He made me bring him here to see the River Diamond."

Just then Dr. Wurst and the museum workers came into the room. They all loaded up plates and sat in a group, eating.

After breakfast, everyone rolled up their sleeping bags and got their stuff together. Mr. Davis and Alex walked over to say good-bye.

"Let's keep in touch," Dink's father said. He and Mr. Davis exchanged email addresses and phone numbers.

Mr. Davis handed Dink's father his book of crossword puzzles. "I didn't get to do any puzzles," he said.

"Oh, I need to return your anagram book," Dink's father said. "Do you have it, Dink?"

"Yup," Dink said. "In my backpack."

"Keep it," Mr. Davis said. "I have plenty more at home."

Dink felt someone tug his shirt. It was Alex, holding one of his books. He pulled Dink a few yards away from the others.

Alex had on a baggy sweatshirt and jeans. His sneaker laces were untied, and his glasses were so smudged Dink didn't know how the kid could read anything through them.

"What's going on, Alex?" Dink asked.

"It's fake!" Alex whispered.

CHAPTER 6

Dink looked down into the kid's anxious face. "What is?" he asked.

"The River Diamond," Alex said. "It isn't a diamond at all!"

"It's not?" Dink said.

Alex's head shook left and right. His hair was still messy from last night. He held up a book. "It's a fake diamond, and I can prove it!"

Josh and Ruth Rose walked over.

"What's happening?" Josh asked.

"Alex just told me the River Diamond isn't real," Dink said quietly.

"Oh yeah?" Josh said. "Well, then what is it?"

"It's something else that's hard, like concrete," Alex said. "It might be mixed with mud. And the shiny parts could be chunks of black plastic."

"How do you know, Alex?" Ruth Rose asked. "Dr. Wurst thinks it's the River Diamond."

Alex pushed his glasses higher on his nose. "When we got here yesterday, I looked at the River Diamond through my magnifying glass," he said. "*That* one was a real diamond!"

"So how is this one a fake?" Josh asked, nodding his head toward the other room.

"There's a scratch mark on one side of it, where the shiny black stuff shows through the mud," Alex said. "A *big* scratch, and it wasn't there before. Yesterday, I mean."

"Well, that plank fell right on it,"

Dink said. "That could have scratched the diamond, right?"

Alex shook his head. "Uh-uh." He opened his book and pointed to a page. "It says right here, real diamonds are very hard. You can't scratch them unless you do it with another diamond."

The kids huddled and read the paragraph above Alex's finger.

Dink turned around. The parents were busy saying good-bye to each other and to Sylvia and Dr. Wurst. "Can you show us the scratch?" he asked Alex.

"Sure," Alex said. "Come on."

Dink, Josh, and Ruth Rose followed him into the Spino room. They walked past the colossal fossil and stopped at the River Diamond display dome.

Alex whipped his magnifying glass out of a pocket and handed it to Dink. "Look on that side, closest to Spino."

Dink took the glass and leaned over the fence to get as close as he could.

"Don't touch it, dude!" Josh said. "That alarm will go off again!"

"I'm not touching anything," Dink said. He peered through Alex's magnifying glass, making the diamond seem much bigger than its actual size. This made it easy for Dink to see a two-inch-long scratch along one edge.

He backed away and looked at Alex. "There *is* a scratch," he said.

"I told you," Alex said.

"But . . . I don't get it," Dink said. He handed the magnifying glass to Ruth Rose, who also studied the scratch mark. "If the board fell on the real diamond, it wouldn't make a scratch, right, Alex?"

Alex nodded. "Wood couldn't scratch a real diamond," he said.

"Does that mean the diamond we found stuck under the board last night *wasn't* the real River Diamond?" Josh asked.

Dink nodded. "I guess so," he said.

"But Sylvia picked it up, and they took it to Dr. Wurst's office," Ruth Rose said. "*He* must have thought it was the real River Diamond!"

"He didn't get a good look at the diamond, though," Dink said. "Remember, Sylvia just grabbed it, and they went right into his office. If Alex is right, the diamond Sylvia picked up was a fake. And now it's here, inside the dome."

"I have another idea," Josh said. "What if the one we found under the plank last night *was* the real River Diamond? Sylvia carried the real diamond into Dr. Wurst's office. Then, this morning, he put this fake one under the dome and kept the real one."

"Why would he do that?" Dink asked.

Josh grinned. "Because it's worth five million dollars!"

"*What?*" Dink said. "You think Dr. Wurst is trying to steal the River Diamond?"

Josh just looked at Dink and shrugged. "Maybe it was Dr. Wurst who made the plank crash into the dome so he could get the diamond," he said. "That's why he was so mad when he thought you almost got it first."

"But Dr. Wurst wasn't even in the museum last night until after the alarm went off," Ruth Rose said.

"Dink? Guys?" Dink's father said from behind them. "We're ready to go. I have to be at my meeting in a couple of hours. Say good-bye to Alex."

Everyone dragged their backpacks and sleeping bags past Spino, through the museum, and out the door. Sylvia and the other chaperones thanked them for coming, and the kids all thanked them for a fun sleepover.

"The dino cookies were awesome!" Josh told Sylvia. "I ate four!"

Sylvia smiled. "Only four?" she said.

A lot of the people climbed into taxis.

Some were picked up by cars. Mr. Davis and Alex headed for a subway station.

Dink, his father, Josh, and Ruth Rose walked to their hotel, a few blocks away.

"Well, did you kids have fun?" Dink's father asked.

"It was a blast," Josh said. "Lots of food, and I didn't get eaten by a dinosaur!"

"Thank you, Mr. Duncan," Ruth Rose

said. "I never knew about Spinosaurus before we came here."

"I liked everything," Dink said. "Thanks, Dad!"

"You can explore some of Boston while I'm at my meeting," Mr. Duncan said. "You could go ride on the Swan Boats. Or maybe go see Paul Revere's house."

"I have a guidebook," Ruth Rose

said. "It has a map that shows lots of stuff to do."

"Good," Mr. Duncan said. "My meeting will be out by four, and I'll see you at the hotel around four-thirty."

At the hotel, the kids dropped off their packs and sleeping bags. Dink's father handed him some money. "Got your cell phone?" he asked.

Dink patted his pocket. "Yup."

"Good! Now you guys go see Boston, and I'm headed for a hot shower!"

Dink, Josh, and Ruth Rose walked out onto the street.

"We've got lots of time till four-thirty," Dink said. "Know what I want to do?"

"Tell us," Josh said.

"Find the River Diamond," Dink answered. "The *real* one."

CHAPTER 7

Josh and Ruth Rose stared at him.

"I know it's crazy," Dink said. "But Alex convinced me that the diamond we saw yesterday was the real deal. So if the diamond under the dome is a fake, what happened to the one we saw yesterday?"

"I still think Dr. Wurst stole the real River Diamond," Josh said. "Then he shoved the fake diamond under the plank so people would think the plank fell on it, and that's what made the scratch."

"But when could he have done it,

Josh?" Ruth Rose insisted. "Dr. Wurst left the museum last night."

Josh wiggled his eyebrows. "He could have snuck back in after we were all asleep," he said.

The kids sat on a bench. A pigeon flew over and landed at their feet.

Dink said, "Well, *someone* made that plank crash into the diamond case to steal the diamond. Josh is right: whoever took the real diamond stuck that phony one under the plank."

"And you think we can find the real one?" Ruth Rose asked. "How?"

Dink grinned. "I have a clue."

He pulled the anagram book from his pocket and showed Ruth Rose and Josh the three black hairs.

"Remember these?" Dink asked.

"Sure, I found them on your shirt last night," Josh said.

"Right," Dink said, "and I think they got *onto* my shirt when we were trying to shove that plank off the diamond.

I mean off the fake diamond. I think the hairs were on the plank before they were on my shirt."

"Okay," Josh said. "So?"

"So what if the hairs came from the person who made the plank fall onto the diamond case?" Dink said. He put the hairs and the book back in his pocket. "When the thief lifted the plank to wedge the fake diamond under it, he must have left these hairs behind. Then he ran out of the museum with the real River Diamond."

"But it happened in the middle of the night," Ruth Rose said. "It had to be someone who was in the museum with us, right?"

Dink nodded. "Right," he said. "This morning I met a scientist in the bathroom. He works in the lab there. His name is Trevor. He has black hair."

Dink showed Josh and Ruth Rose the hair he'd found on the bathroom sink.

"I think this hair came from Trevor," he said. "And it looks the same as the three that Josh found on my shirt."

"Sylvia has black hair, too," Josh said.

"Sylvia?" Ruth Rose said. "Could she push that plank off those ladders? It took the *three* of us to move it!"

"She wouldn't have to," Dink said. "Remember, last night one of the guards told us the ladder fell first. The ladder landed on the plank, making it fall. All Sylvia had to do was shove the ladder."

"But if Sylvia didn't touch the plank," Ruth Rose asked, "how could her hair be on it?"

"Her hair could have gotten on the plank when she put the fake diamond under it," Dink said. "*After* it fell."

"What about this Trevor guy?" asked Josh. "Was he in the museum last night?"

Dink shrugged. "Maybe. He could have hidden in the lab all night," he said. "All Trevor would have to do is sneak out real late and make the crash, setting off the alarm. Then he could grab the actual River Diamond when it rolled onto the floor, and leave the fake one under the plank."

"So you think the thief is either Sylvia or Trevor?" Ruth Rose asked.

Dink shrugged. "They both have black hair, and they both could have done it during the night," he said.

"Or it could have been Dr. Wurst," Josh added. "Maybe he came back and hid somewhere until we were sleeping."

"I guess he could have," Ruth Rose agreed.

"Wait a minute!" Josh said. "What if all *three* of them are in on it? Dr. Wurst, Trevor, and Sylvia could have pulled it off together!"

Dink looked at Josh. "How would they do it?" he asked.

Josh closed his eyes for a few seconds. "Okay, here's how. Sylvia waits till we're all asleep, and then she sneaks out of the room and meets Trevor. She has the fake diamond in one of the pockets in her cargo pants.

"She or Trevor shoves the ladder into the plank, and the plank falls. It smashes into the River Diamond dome, and the alarm goes off.

"The River Diamond falls onto the floor, and Trevor grabs it. He sticks the fake diamond under the plank and takes off with the real one. Some of his hair catches on the plank, but he doesn't know it.

"As soon as Trevor is out the door, Sylvia comes in and tells us there was an *accident*."

"But what about Dr. Wurst?" Ruth Rose asked. "He came a few minutes later, and he looked like he'd just gotten out of bed."

"That was part of their plan!" Josh said.

"But Sylvia grabbed the diamond and took it to Dr. Wurst's office," Dink said. "Dr. Wurst thought it was the real one."

"No," Josh said, grinning. "He only *pretended* to think she picked up the real one. If he was partners with Sylvia and Trevor, he *knew* they already had the real diamond. He *knew* she was grabbing the fake. Then, this morning, he put the fake one under the dome."

Dink and Ruth Rose just stared at Josh.

"The three of them would wait awhile," Josh continued, "then sell the River Diamond and split the five million bucks!"

"If you're right, that was brilliant," Ruth Rose said.

"Yup, they get rich, and poor Mr. Alanis gets a hunk of cement and mud," he said.

Dink stood up. "That's why we're going to find the real diamond for him!" he said.

"How?" Josh asked.

"I have an idea," Dink said. "But we have to go back to the museum."

CHAPTER 8

They started walking. "How would anyone be able to make a fake diamond so it looked just like the real River Diamond?" Josh asked.

"Sylvia could probably do it," Ruth Rose said. "She told me she makes jewelry, and she made that bracelet she always wears."

"The real one looked like a dirty hunk of black coal," Dink reminded them. "So the fake one had to look exactly the same."

"Her bracelet has chunks of stone, metal, and plastic in it," Ruth Rose went on.

"Great! Let's go arrest her!" Josh said.

"Slow down, Josh," Dink said. "We have no proof that she did anything, and the same for Trevor and Dr. Wurst."

Josh shook his head. "You're right," he said. "So how do we get proof?"

"I've been thinking about this since I woke up," Dink said. "What if we go see Trevor? I'll show him the hairs we found on my shirt and ask if they're from a man or woman. See what he says."

"How can he tell that?" Ruth Rose asked.

"He's a paleontologist, but he told me he used to be a detective," Dink said. "He knows about clues and stuff."

"Dink, Trevor could be the thief, remember?" Josh said. "The hairs could be *his.* You even said so. If you ask him, he has to lie to us, like *Dude, these hairs are from a dog or a chimpanzee or something.* If Trevor and Sylvia stole the diamond, he'd be crazy to admit that the hairs came from him or her!"

"Maybe, but I want to watch his face when I show him the hairs," Dink said. "Sometimes the bad guy's eyes give it all away."

"I like your idea," Ruth Rose told Dink. "We'll watch Trevor's eyes."

"But what if he really *did* steal the diamond?" Josh asked. "As soon as you show him the hairs, he'll know we suspect him. He could lock us up in a dungeon under the museum!"

Ruth Rose laughed. "I doubt there's a dungeon under the New England Children's Museum," she said.

"Well, there could be," Josh said. "And everyone knows dungeons have tons of spiders!"

Dink grinned. "Let's go find out," he said.

The kids hurried back toward the museum. "I hope Sylvia isn't the thief," Ruth Rose said. "She's so nice! I saw her give a sandwich to a homeless man yesterday."

"I thought Trevor was pretty nice, too," Dink said. "But they both have straight black hair, and they both work at the museum. We know Sylvia was there when the River Diamond got stolen, and maybe he was there, too."

They passed a store that sold toys. The window display was a tall building made of small plastic blocks. In front of the building were miniature cars, trees, children, and dogs, all built from the little blocks.

The next store showed a female mannequin wearing a dark fur coat. A sign next to her said FUR STORAGE. LET US KEEP YOUR BEAUTIFUL FUR COAT SAFE!

"Hey, remember that guy Nog who works at the museum?" Josh asked. "His hair was black. So was his beard!"

"Yeah, but I'm pretty sure his beard

and hair were fake," Dink said. "Besides, they were both curly. The hairs from my shirt are straight. So is the one I found on the sink in the bathroom."

The kids kept walking toward the museum.

"I just thought of something!" Josh said. "I'm so smart!"

Dink and Ruth Rose stopped walking. "Please tell us why you are so smart," Dink said, grinning.

"I just figured out why the thief *has* to be Sylvia," Josh said.

"Why?" Ruth Rose asked.

Josh grinned. "Her last name is Slate, right?" he asked.

Dink and Ruth Rose nodded.

"So an anagram for SLATE is STEAL!"

Dink just shook his head.

Ten minutes later the kids walked up the museum steps. A sign next to the door gave the museum's hours.

"It won't be open for another hour," Ruth Rose said.

Dink saw a button and pushed it. They all heard a loud buzzing sound.

Sylvia opened the door. She smiled when she saw the kids. "Hey," she said. "Have you come back for more cookies?"

MUSEUM HOURS

MON-THURS 10-5

RIDAY 10-7

AT-SUN

NECM

Sylvia wasn't wearing her cap. Dink stared at her hair. It was shiny, black, and straight.

"Um, no," Dink said. "But they were really good. We came to see Trevor. Is he here?"

"My brother?" Sylvia asked. "Sure, he's in his lab."

Her brother! Dink thought. "Can you ask him if we can talk to him?" he said.

Sylvia stared at Dink for a minute. "Okay. Come on in," she said.

They stepped inside the lobby, and Sylvia locked the door behind them. She walked them to the lab door and knocked, then opened it and slipped inside.

Everything in the exhibit looked the way it had yesterday. The boxes of Spinosaurus bones were laid out neatly against a wall. The River Diamond display looked as if it had never been disturbed. No one else suspected that the diamond under the dome was a fake.

The kids stood beneath Spino and waited. Dink looked up at the plank that had fallen last night. Could it fall again? He took a few steps backward.

"Did you hear what she said?" Josh hissed. "They're brother and sister! It's a family crime! Dr. Wurst is probably their father!"

Ruth Rose giggled. "Too much TV, Josh," she whispered.

Just then Trevor and Sylvia came out of the lab. When Dink saw them together, he could tell they were related. Their hair was the same, and they both had blue eyes.

"Hey, Dink," Trevor said. "You wanted to see me?"

Suddenly Dink felt scared to ask Trevor about the hairs. What if Trevor and Sylvia *were* the thieves?

Dink thought about how fast he and Josh and Ruth Rose could run for the exit if they had to. But could they unlock the door?

"We wanted to know if we could see your lab," Ruth Rose piped up.

"My lab?" Trevor asked. "Why?"

Dink still didn't know what to say.

"Because I want to be a scientist!" Josh blurted out. "When I told my teacher we were coming here, he asked me to interview someone who works in a lab. I need to learn about clues and fingerprints and stuff."

Trevor smiled. "Cool," he said. "Okay, come on in. See you later, Sis."

Good, Dink thought. *Josh figured out a way to ask about the hairs.*

Sylvia gave her brother a long look, then headed for the office. Trevor led the kids toward the lab door.

Dink's legs felt like rubber bands. Even with his hands stuck in his pockets, they were cold. He felt his cell phone and wished he had let his dad know where they were.

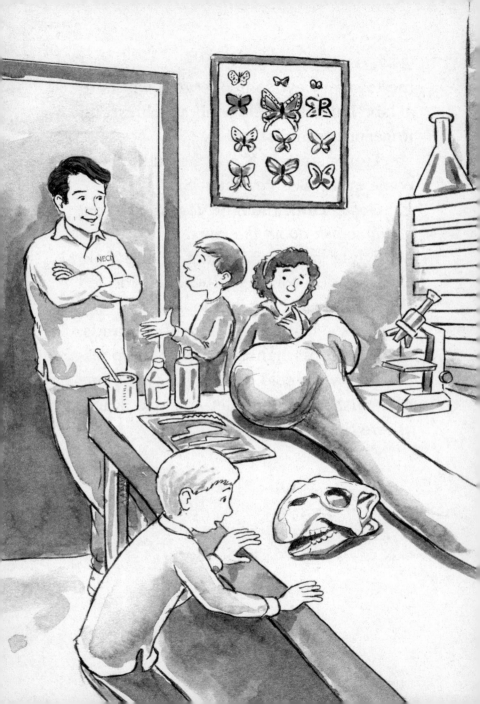

CHAPTER 9

After the kids were in the lab, Trevor closed the door and leaned against it. He folded his thick arms over his chest. "Okay, ask away," he said.

We're trapped, Dink thought. And there were no windows.

"Why did you become a scientist?" Josh asked Trevor.

"I like to study things," Trevor answered. "I want to know what makes the universe work. I like to solve problems."

Dink looked around the room. Everything was white and very clean. Like a hospital. On top of a stainless steel table, he saw a microscope, bottles filled with different-colored liquids, and a long bone. Next to the bone was a row of sharp knives.

"Um, you told Dink you were a detective once," Josh said.

Trevor nodded. "I studied criminology in college," he said. "Thought I'd have fun catching bad guys, but it wasn't much fun at all. Now I study old bones and try to imagine what the real beast looked like, what it ate, and how it lived and died."

Dink glanced at Trevor's neatly combed black hair. *Did three of those hairs end up on my shirt?* he wondered. *Did Trevor shove the fake diamond under that heavy board?*

"Did you learn how to take fingerprints when you were a detective?" Ruth Rose asked.

"Yup."

Dink took a deep breath, then asked

his question. "Can you tell where a hair came from? I mean, from a certain man or woman?"

"Sometimes," Trevor said. "It depends on how complete the hair is. The shaft of the hair is the part we can see. On our heads, the shafts are what we shampoo and comb. But under the scalp, on the end of each hair shaft, there's something called a *follicle*. This follicle has a tiny bulb that attaches the shaft to the skin. Scientists can study a follicle and learn a lot about the person the hair came from."

Dink took the paper towel from his pocket and laid it on the table. He unwrapped it so they could all see the black hair against the white paper. Then he took the first three hairs from the anagram book and laid them next to the others on the paper towel.

"Where'd you get those?" Trevor asked.

Dink blinked. He didn't want to lie. "I . . ."

"They're part of a mystery we're try-ing to solve," Ruth Rose said. "We love mysteries. It's sort of a hobby for us!"

Dink swallowed. *Thank you, Ruth Rose!*

Trevor picked up the paper towel and held it close to his eyes. "Hmmm," he said.

He stepped over to the microscope and slid the hairs onto a little glass tray. He sat in a chair and adjusted the micro-scope while looking through the eye-piece at the hairs. "I thought so," he said. "Come take a look."

Dink moved over, and Trevor stood up. "Kneel in the chair so you can see," he told Dink. "Keep both eyes open, but put one against the little rubber cup."

Dink followed Trevor's instructions. At first all he saw was a dark blur. "It looks all fuzzy," he said.

Trevor adjusted a knob. "Better?" he asked.

Dink pulled back. "Yes! One of the hairs looks like a tree branch with bark!" he said. "I can see the follicle thing on the end! The other three hairs are different. They're smoother."

Trevor smiled. He removed the four hairs and placed them back on the paper towel. "Finding hairs at a crime scene is one way detectives can arrest the right person," he explained. "They compare the follicles and the shafts. Only one of the four hairs you gave me is from a human head."

Trevor folded the paper towel and handed it back to Dink. "The other three aren't even real hair," he said. "They're man-made, which means they don't have follicles and never grew out of skin."

The three kids just stared at him.

"Then where did they come from?" Ruth Rose asked.

Trevor shrugged. "Probably from an article of clothing," he said. "Gloves, a jacket, a fake fur collar, maybe."

A thought was buzzing around Dink's brain, like a bee in a bottle.

The kids thanked Trevor and left the lab. "Well, Mr. Detective," Josh said to Dink. "What do you think? Did Trevor's eyes tell you he stole the River Diamond?"

"He could have," Dink said. "But now we know the hairs you found on my shirt aren't *Trevor's* hairs."

"They aren't *anyone's* hairs," Ruth Rose said. "They're fake—like the diamond is fake."

The kids walked through the Spino room. Dink stopped and gazed up at

Spino's head, which almost touched the ceiling. The workers were sitting together, taking a coffee break.

"He saw it all," Dink said.

Josh was standing next to Dink. "Who, Trevor?" he asked.

"No, Spino," Dink said. "He saw what really happened last night before the alarm went off. Spino saw who shoved the ladder, making the plank fall on top of the diamond case. Spino saw who stole the River Diamond and left that fake one."

"Too bad dinosaurs can't talk like the ones in that movie last night," Josh said.

Ruth Rose walked over to the River Diamond exhibit. "But we don't know for sure if this *is* a fake," she said, peering through the dome. "Couldn't it be the real River Diamond, and Alex is wrong?"

Dink joined her and looked through the dome. "I think Alex is right," he said.

"The plank couldn't scratch a real diamond, but it could scratch a fake one. And this one definitely has a scratch on one side."

"Now we just have to figure out how fake hairs got on that plank," Ruth Rose said.

"Even if they're not human hairs," Josh said, "they still could have dropped off a human."

"How?" Ruth Rose asked.

Josh shrugged. "Maybe the thief works in a place that makes fake fur coats," he said. "He might have some of the fake fur on his body. Or maybe the crook was wearing gorilla gloves when he moved the plank to—"

"Oh my gosh!" Dink said. "Nog was wearing a caveman costume! The wig and beard were curly, but that coat thing had straight black hair all over it! And I'll bet it was fake fur!"

CHAPTER 10

"You're right!" Josh said. "I saw a movie once where some thieves were dressed like apes. Their costumes looked just like the one Nog was wearing!"

"If *Nog* lifted the plank or shoved it, some of the hairs from his costume could have been left behind!" Ruth Rose said. "Then when *we* shoved the plank, the hairs got onto your shirt!"

"But I don't think Nog was here last night," Dink said. "Did anyone see him?"

"I didn't," Ruth Rose said. "But he could have been hiding somewhere, just like Trevor could have been hiding."

"And then he creeps out in the middle of the night," Dink added. "He makes the plank fall, grabs the River Diamond, and leaves the fake one. I like it!"

"But I thought we decided it was Trevor, Sylvia, and Dr. Wurst?" Josh said.

"That was before Trevor told us the hairs were fake," Dink said.

"But what if he's lying?" Josh asked. "What if Trevor realized the hairs were really his and knew we were onto him?"

"I think he was telling the truth," Ruth Rose said. "I was watching his eyes. They didn't look sneaky. His eyes looked interested in what he was telling us."

"And I saw the hairs under the microscope," Dink said. "The one I found in the bathroom was different from the three you found on my shirt. Trevor was combing his hair over the sink, so that hair was probably from his head. The other three weren't his, so maybe he never touched that plank."

"Okay, so now what do we do?" Josh asked.

Dink walked toward the office. "We find Nog, but I'm guessing that isn't his real name," he said.

"A fake name, fake hairs, and a fake diamond," Josh said.

"If we can get some hairs from Nog's costume, we can see if they're the same as the ones that came from the plank and my shirt," Dink said. "That would at least prove that Nog was messing with the plank."

"Maybe we'll catch him with the diamond!" Josh said.

"What about fingerprints?" Ruth Rose asked. "If we got Nog's fingerprints, the police could see if the same fingerprints were on the fake diamond. If his fingerprints *are* on the fake, doesn't that prove he's the thief?"

"Right," Dink said.

"How do we get his fingerprints?" Josh asked.

"I'll think of something," Ruth Rose said. "First we have to *find* him!"

Dink knocked on the office door.

Sylvia opened the door. "Hi, kids," she said. "Was Trevor any help?"

"He was a lot of help," Dink said. "We learned about how detectives can catch crooks by finding their hair."

Sylvia touched her own hair. "So . . . ?"

"Trevor told us about artificial hair, too," Ruth Rose added. "Like that caveman costume Nog was wearing yesterday. We'd like to talk to him about . . . our project."

"Is Nog his real name?" Dink asked.

Sylvia laughed. "No, his name is Jack."

"Do you know where he lives?" Josh asked.

"Nope, he's never told me," Sylvia said.

"He told us he lives near Paul Revere's house," Ruth Rose said.

"Oh, that's a museum," Sylvia said.

"Is it close enough to walk?" Ruth Rose asked.

Sylvia shook her head. "Not really," she said. "But you can walk to where they park the Swan Boats. You'll find a bus stop there. Wait for one that says *Paul Revere House* on the little sign. If you see Jack, ask him why he didn't come to work today!"

The kids walked to the Swan Boat pond, then waited about ten minutes for the Paul Revere House bus. Dink paid with some of the money his dad had given him, and they took seats up front.

"It's pretty cool to think Paul Revere hung out around here," Josh said. "He might have ridden on this same bus. Maybe he sat in this seat!"

Dink laughed. "Josh, Paul Revere

died almost two hundred years ago," he said. "In those days, people rode on horses, not buses."

"I knew that, Matt," Josh said, making goofy eyes at Dink. "Just playing with you."

The bus stopped in front of a dark brown house. A small sign said Paul Revere lived in the house starting in 1770.

The kids left the bus and walked toward the house. It was squeezed between some other old buildings. Another bus pulled up, and a bunch of tourists climbed down. They walked up the sidewalk toward the house.

Dink saw a restaurant, a dry-cleaning place, and a flower shop. "Maybe we should ask if anyone knows where Jack lives," he said.

They were heading for the flower shop when they passed a bright yellow door. Ruth Rose said, "Wait!" She pointed to a sign that said YOUR FANTASY—RENT COSTUMES FOR ALL OCCASIONS. "If Jack lives near here, maybe he got his caveman costume from this shop!"

In the window, they saw Elvis, a clown, and Mickey Mouse. "Come on," Ruth Rose said.

Inside the shop, costumes hung from hooks on the walls. They saw princesses, movie stars, even a giant chicken.

"Can I help you?" a man asked from behind the counter.

The kids stepped up to the counter. "Do you have a caveman costume?" Dink asked.

The man nodded. "Sure do," he said. "But I'm afraid it's for adult sizes. Way too big for you."

"Can we see it anyway?" Ruth Rose asked.

"Sure," he said. "It was rented for a long time, but it just came back this morning."

The man went behind a curtain and returned a few minutes later with a large, flat box. He removed the lid and laid it on the counter in front of Dink. Inside the box, the kids saw Nog's fake fur coat, shaggy beard and wig, and club, which turned out to be made of cardboard.

"That's what Nog, I mean Jack, was wearing!" Ruth Rose said.

Dink noticed a few black hairs on the inside of the box lid. He wet a finger, picked up one of the hairs, and slipped it into his pocket.

"Do you kids know Jack?" the man asked.

"Yes, we met him at the New England Children's Museum!" Ruth Rose said. "He was wearing this, and he said he lived near Paul Revere's house. We want to talk to him about . . . a mystery we're trying to solve."

The man nodded. "Jack rented this

caveman outfit for his job at the museum," he said. "I don't know why he brought it back so soon. Maybe he got fired!"

Or if he stole the River Diamond, worth millions of dollars, maybe he quit! Dink thought. *And that's why he returned the costume!*

CHAPTER 11

"Can you tell us where he lives?" Ruth Rose asked.

The man walked over to the front window and pointed. "See that red-brick building?" he asked. "He's in one of those apartments."

The kids thanked him and left his store. They walked toward the brick apartment building. There was a small window on each side of the door.

Dink pulled the paper towel from his pocket. He placed the hair he'd taken from the costume box next to the other hairs. "I think it's the same as the other three," he said. "All from Nog's costume."

"And three of the four hairs were on that plank," Ruth Rose added. "So—"

"So it must have been Nog who made the plank fall," Josh interrupted. "Then he stuck the fake diamond under the plank, leaving the hairs behind. Nog is the thief!"

The three kids stared at the apartment building. The windows made Dink think of eyes, watching him. And Jack might be somewhere in that building. "Is anyone else scared?" Dink asked.

The kids climbed up the cement steps and looked at the name tags next to the door. "This one says Jack Rapp," Ruth Rose said. "With the letter B after his name."

A woman came up behind them with an armload of grocery bags. "Can I help you?" she asked.

"We're looking for Jack," Dink told her.

"Down those stairs," she said, pointing with her chin because her hands were full of bags. "He's in the basement apartment next to that lilac bush. Now, if I could just get my keys!"

"Can we hold your bags for you?" Ruth Rose asked.

"That would be lovely!" the woman said. She handed her grocery bags to the kids and fished in a pocket for her keys.

When the door was open, she took back the bags. "If Jack isn't home, try looking in the backyard. He has a sort of studio there. He's some kind of artist."

"What does he make?" Dink asked.

"I'm not sure," the woman said. "Jack is very private. I've never been inside his little shed."

The kids went down the basement steps and rang the bell for Jack Rapp. They heard it ring inside, but no one came to the door.

"Guys, what do we say to him if he answers the door?" Ruth Rose asked.

Dink pulled his cell phone from his pocket. "I'll ask him to take a selfie with us," he said.

Josh giggled. "Why do you want a selfie of a man who pretends to be a caveman, who might be a diamond thief?" he asked.

"I'll say it's for our school mystery project," Dink said. "Then we'll have his fingerprints on my phone!"

But no one answered the door.

"Let's try the studio," Ruth Rose said. They walked to the sidewalk, then around the side of the building. Out back they found a yard with a lot of trees, some thick bushes, and one rusty lawn chair. Off to one side, a trash barrel stood in a circle of bare ground near a small garden where tiny green shoots were sprouting.

The studio was on the other side of

the trees and bushes. It was just an old wooden shed. There were no windows, only a narrow door. The door was held open with a shovel propped under the knob. Inside, the kids saw boxes and bottles on a workbench. A lightbulb hung over the bench, shining on a row of tools hanging on the wall.

A man walked past the door. The kids couldn't see his face, but he had short blond hair in a buzz cut.

"Is that him?" Dink whispered.

"I don't know," Ruth Rose said. The man wore jeans, a green sweatshirt, and leather sandals. "Wait, I think it is! He's wearing the same sandals Nog had on yesterday!"

"Now what?" Josh whispered. They were standing in the trees, where they couldn't be seen from the shed. "You still want that selfie, Dink?"

Just then the man they thought was Jack walked out into the yard, carrying a small box. He walked over to the trash barrel and tossed the box in.

The kids froze. If he looked up, he'd see them in the trees.

"Get down!" Dink whispered. They knelt behind the bushes and watched the man return to the shed. He stepped inside, pulled the string to shut off the light, then came back out.

The kids watched him lean the shovel against the shed wall and pull the door closed. He crossed the yard and disappeared down some stairs at the back of the apartment building.

Dink had been holding his breath, and he let it out.

"What do we do now?" Josh asked.

"We get inside," Ruth Rose said. "Come on, guys!" She slipped through the trees, heading for the shed.

"Where are you going?" Josh yelped. "What if he looks out and sees us?"

Dink started after Ruth Rose, pulling Josh along with him. "I checked. There aren't any windows at the back of the apartments," he told Josh. "We can get in and out real fast."

The kids crowded into the shed. Dink quickly closed the door behind them. "Don't turn on the light," he whispered.

"Don't need it," Ruth Rose said. She pulled her flashlight from her backpack and turned it on, aiming the beam at the workbench. They saw chunks of wood, stone, and plastic in different colors. They saw carving knives and other small tools. There were three buckets on the floor. One was half-filled with sand, one held gray powder, and the third contained water.

Dink put his finger into the powder, then took a close look. "I think it's cement," he said. "Alex told us he thought the fake diamond could be partly concrete. If you add sand, gravel, and water to cement, it dries as concrete."

"How do you know that?" Josh asked.

"I helped my dad fix our basement steps," Dink said. Then he grinned and added, "Plus, I'm smart, Art!"

"If Jack stole the River Diamond, maybe it's hidden in here someplace," Ruth Rose said.

They started opening boxes and peering inside the large bottles. Dink got on his knees and searched under the bench. All he found were spiderwebs and dust.

"This is making me pretty nervous," Josh said. "What if Jack catches us and locks us in here? There must be spiders everywhere!"

"One more minute," Dink said. He spied a sweatshirt hanging from a hook on the back of the door. A flyer was sticking out of the pouch pocket. The flyer looked familiar, so he pulled it out.

"Look, guys," Dink said. It was a flyer for the museum sleepover. "I'll bet Jack planned to steal the diamond when he knew there'd be a lot of people around. He must have figured one of the parents or chaperones would get blamed."

Ruth Rose found a small knife on the bench. She wrapped it in a tissue and put it in her backpack. She shut off her flashlight. "Okay, let's go," she said.

"Peek out first," Josh said. "He could be waiting!"

Dink opened the door a crack and looked into the yard. "Okay, let's take off, and fast!"

The kids slipped through the door, and Dink pulled it shut. The yard was empty. He motioned for Josh and Ruth Rose to follow him.

"Wait," Ruth Rose said. Dink looked back and saw her crouching down. "Hey, guys, look at this!"

She pointed to the sharp edge of the shovel that was leaning against the shed. "That's dirt on the shovel," she said. She put a finger on the clump. "It's still damp."

"Maybe he was planting something in his garden," Josh said.

"Or *burying* something in his garden," Ruth Rose said.

CHAPTER 12

Ruth Rose ran over to the garden. She crouched between two rows of tiny green sprouts. Dink and Josh followed her. "What are you looking for?" Dink asked.

"Checking out the dirt around these baby plants," she said. She bent over and took a pinch of the soil. "See, it's black, but the dirt stuck to the shovel is brown."

"So where was he digging?" Josh asked.

They looked around the yard near the shed. Dink's eyes fell on the trash barrel. "That part of the yard has brown dirt. Let's check over there," he said, starting toward the barrel.

The kids studied the ground, but it was hard and packed down. There were no signs of fresh digging.

"What are these marks from?" Josh asked. He was pointing to a big scrape mark in the dirt.

Dink looked at the scrape, then at the trash barrel standing a few feet away. The scrape mark ended at the side of the barrel. "If someone dragged the barrel across the ground, it would make a mark like that," he said.

Dink leaned against the barrel. It

was half-filled with stuff, and heavy. "Help me move this thing," he said to Josh and Ruth Rose.

Josh looked at the barrel. "Why?" he asked.

"I have an idea!" Dink said. "Come on, help me!"

The three kids shoved the barrel aside. Underneath they saw brown earth that looked like it had been recently dug.

"It's the same color as the dirt on the shovel!" Ruth Rose said.

Dink ran over to the shed and grabbed the shovel. He came back and used it to move some of the loose soil where the barrel had been standing. The second time Dink dug in, the shovel hit something hard. He and Josh got on their knees and dug with their hands.

Dink pulled out a white plastic bag. It was covering a round object. Dink quickly unwrapped the bag and looked inside. Then he grinned. "Guess what's in—"

"HEY, WHAT ARE YOU KIDS DOING?" a voice yelled.

Dink, Josh, and Ruth Rose looked up and saw Jack racing across the yard toward them.

"Run!" Dink yelled.

The kids tore around the side of the apartment building. Dink stuffed the white bag inside his shirt so he wouldn't drop it.

Across the street, a bus stood in front of the Paul Revere House. About a dozen tourists were walking toward the house.

"Get on the bus!" Ruth Rose yelled. The three kids bolted across the street and leaped up the bus steps. They were out of breath.

"Sorry, kids," the driver said. "I don't leave for another thirty minutes."

"There's a man chasing us!" Josh croaked out.

"What man?" the driver asked.

"Him!" Ruth Rose said. She pointed

out the window just as Jack charged across the street.

"Shut the door!" Dink said.

Jack reached the bus and was about to leap up the steps when the door closed in his face. He banged on the door, pointing at the kids. "They stole something of mine!" he screamed at the driver. "Open this door!"

"Don't open it, please!" Ruth Rose said.

"Who is that guy?" the driver asked the kids.

"He's a crazy caveman!" Josh croaked, throwing himself down into a seat.

"What's going on here?" the driver asked. "Do I need to call the police?"

"No! Take us to the New England Children's Museum!" Ruth Rose said.

Dink opened the bag and showed the River Diamond to the bus driver. "That guy stole this from the museum yesterday!" Dink said. "We found it buried in his yard!"

"It's worth five million bucks!" Josh said.

"We have to get it back to the museum!" Ruth Rose said.

The driver glanced out at Jack, standing on the sidewalk with a red face and angry, bulging eyes. "Okay, sit down and buckle up!"

Dink and Ruth Rose fell into seats next to Josh and clicked their seat belts. "I'm never going to another museum in my life!" Josh moaned.

The bus driver pulled away from the Paul Revere House. Through the bus windows, the kids watched Jack become smaller and smaller.

Ten minutes later Dink, Josh, and Ruth Rose ran up the museum steps, through the lobby, and into the room with the colossal fossil. Sylvia was showing some people the Spinosaurus skeleton. Her eyes went wide when she saw the kids running toward her.

They stopped at the diamond display case. The dome was empty. "Oh no!" Dink said. He motioned for Sylvia to come over.

She excused herself from her group and joined the kids. "What's going on?" she asked. "You three look like you've seen a ghost!"

"Can we talk to Dr. Wurst?" Dink whispered. "It's real important!"

"Sorry, he's busy," Sylvia said. "He's returning the River Diamond to Mr. Alanis today. They're taking pictures for the newspaper! Can I help you with something?"

"He can't do that!" Dink cried. "The River Diamond is a fake!"

He held open the white bag, and Sylvia looked inside. "What is that?" she asked. "It looks like the River Diamond!"

"It *is* the River Diamond!" Dink said. "The *real* one. The one that was under the dome this morning is fake!"

"Nog, I mean Jack, stole the real one last night," Josh said. "We found where he hid it, and we're bringing it back!"

"What? I don't understand," Sylvia said. "We found the River Diamond on the floor after the alarm went off, right over there!"

"Jack made that plank fall last night," Dink explained. "He did it to crack open the display. Then he took the River Diamond—this one—and left a fake one where you would find it and think *that* was the real one!"

Sylvia reached into the bag and gently picked up what was inside. She held the real River Diamond close. "Remarkable," she said.

"We saw Jack's studio, where he made the fake diamond!" Josh said.

Sylvia looked at the kids. "I think

I'd better disturb them," she said. She placed the River Diamond back in the white bag, took the bag from Dink, and walked toward the office.

A minute later they were all in Dr. Wurst's office. The two "diamonds" sat side by side on his desk. He and Mr. Alanis were staring at the two objects. A newspaper photographer was taking pictures of the scene.

"Well, you sure could have fooled me," Mr. Alanis said. "The two are very much alike. But seeing them next to each other, I can tell that one is carefully handmade from concrete, mud, and other things. It was made to look old and muddy, like the real one."

"I was totally fooled, too," Sylvia said. "I walked past the fake one at least fifty times today, thinking it was the real River Diamond."

"I'm afraid the thief got this past all

of us," Dr. Wurst said. He smiled at the kids. "How did you know?"

"I'm pretty sure Jack Rapp shoved the ladder into the plank last night so it would crash into the River Diamond," Dink said. "Then he stole the real diamond and left this fake one."

The kids showed them the scratch that Alex had noticed on the fake River Diamond. They explained how they thought the heavy plank had made the scratch mark. And how Josh had found hairs from Jack's fake fur costume on Dink's shirt. They told him about their trip to Jack's house and what they found there.

Dr. Wurst shook his head. "Amazing," he said. "But how did you know Jack had hidden the River Diamond in his yard?"

"He was sneaky!" Josh said. "He buried it under his trash barrel!"

Ruth Rose told Dr. Wurst how she'd noticed the soil on the shovel. "It was a different color from the dirt in his garden," she said.

Sylvia smiled at Ruth Rose. "Let me know if you ever want a job in my brother's lab," she said.

"Can we have Jack arrested?" Mr. Alanis asked.

"I'm not sure I can ask the police to pick him up without proof," Dr. Wurst said. "He could deny everything and tell us he had no idea how that bag got under his trash barrel."

"I know how to prove he took it," Ruth Rose said. She opened her backpack and pulled out the knife she'd taken from Jack's workbench, wrapped in the tissue. "I took this from his shed," she said. "It will have Jack's fingerprints on it. His prints might also be on the ladder!"

"Perhaps we'll find his prints on this plastic bag, too," Dr. Wurst said.

He picked up his cell phone and

tapped a few keys. "Trevor," he said into his phone, "can you please come to my office?"

Trevor was easily able to find Jack's prints on the shiny knife handle. Using special tape, he was able to lift the prints, then get more prints from the smooth parts of the fake diamond.

"Hmmm," Trevor said. "I see three different people's prints here."

"Some will be Sylvia's and mine," Dr. Wurst said. "Remember, we brought the fake diamond here to my office last night. I put it in my safe, thinking it was the real one!"

The other prints matched the ones from Jack's knife.

"Then there's no question," Dr. Wurst said. "Jack Rapp is our thief." He took out his cell phone again and called the police.

Mr. Alanis picked up the fake diamond. "To think I was going to take this to a jeweler," he said. "I might have ended up in jail!"

He looked at the kids. "You three have saved me from embarrassment and from losing millions of dollars," he said. "Thank you!"

"How about a picture?" the photographer asked. He aimed his camera at the group and the two diamonds.

After the picture, Josh grinned and licked his lips. "Are there any more of those dino cookies?" he asked.

DID YOU FIND THE
SECRET MESSAGE
HIDDEN IN THIS BOOK?

If you *don't* want
to know the answer,
don't look at the bottom
of this page!

Answer:
SPINO WANTS ANOTHER SLEEPOVER!

Craig Norton

ABOUT THE AUTHOR

Ron Roy has been writing books for children since 1974. He is the author of dozens of books, including the popular A to Z Mysteries®, Calendar Mysteries, and Capital Mysteries. When not working on a new book, Ron likes to teach his dog tricks, play poker with friends, travel, and read thrilling mystery books.